No Help at All

Greenwillow
Read-alone

No Help at All

by **Betty Baker**

pictures by **Emily Arnold McCully**

GREENWILLOW BOOKS

A Division of William Morrow & Company, Inc., New York

Library of Congress Cataloging in Publication Data
Baker, Betty.
No help at all. (Greenwillow read-alone)
Summary: In return for saving a boy's life,
a Mayan rain god expects some help around his house—
but the boy is really no help at all.
1. Mayas—Legends.   2.   Indians of Mexico—
Legends.   3.   Indians of Central America—Legends.
[1.   Mayas—Legends.   2.   Indians of Mexico—Legends.
3.   Folklore—Mexico]   I.   McCully, Emily Arnold
II.   Title.   F1435.3.F6B27   398.2   76-13223
ISBN 0-688-80056-4   ISBN 0-688-84056-6 lib. bdg.

West Chac
lived in the sky
over the land
of the Maya.

Three other chacs
lived in the sky.
Each had a house
under a big tree.

Each had a bag

to hold the wind,

a stone ax to make

thunder and lightning

and a pot to carry rain.

When people below
wanted rain, they called
to one of the chacs.
They gave the chac food.
Then they asked him
to ride the clouds
and spill the rain.

But they did not call
to West Chac.
"West Rain," said the people,
"is not good for corn."

West Chac's house was black.

His tree was black

and his garden grew black corn.

He had a loom
that made black clouds.
There was a turtle to sit on
or to hold down the loom
and a magic pan
that cooked his food.

Frogs and toads

were his friends.

They liked to sing with him,

but West Chac had no time.

No one asked him

to spill the rain.

No one gave him food.

All summer long

West Chac had to work

in his garden.

Sometimes in winter
he rode the clouds
and let some of the wind
out of the bag.

But in the summer
he had the garden
to care for.
He did not have time
to sit on the turtle
and sing with his friends.
"I need help," he said.
But the other chacs
had work to do, too.

One day West Chac

was pulling yams.

He heard, "Help! Help!"

He pulled up a yam

and looked under it.

Down below,

a boy climbed a tree.

He climbed to get away

from a man-eating thing.

But the Thing

was climbing the tree.

"Help!" said the boy.

"Some one help me!"

West Chac said, "If I help you,

then you must help me."

"For how long?" said the boy.

"For as long as I say."

"That could be always,"

said the boy.

"Yes, it could," said West Chac.

The boy said, "No."

Then he said, "Oh, ow!

Yes! I will help you

for as long as you say."

West Chac put down a rope.

The rope grew

until the boy took it.

West Chac pulled him up.

"Now," said the chac,

"you can help me."

"No," said the boy.

"Now I must eat."

West Chac told him,

"Go in the house.

Tell the pan

to give you a corn cake."

The boy thought,

I can eat more

then one corn cake.

He told the pan,

"Give me many corn cakes."

And the pan did.

"Help! Help!" said the boy.

West Chac had to run
and stop the pan.
"That did not help me,"
he said.
"It made more to do."

"I will clean the house,"
said the boy.
"Good," said West Chac.
"I will ask my friends
to eat and sing with me."

The boy made the house
neat and clean.
He put down new mats
and took away the old ones.
When he came back,
the house was full
of frogs and toads.
"Get out!" he told them.
They did not want to go,
but he took the broom
and made them get out.

"Where are my friends?" said West Chac.

The boy said, "No one was here.

Just a lot of toads and frogs

in the clean house.

It took a long time

to get them all out."

"You put out my friends,"

said West Chac.

"What kind of help is that?"

"But I cleaned the house,"

said the boy.

"But I need help
in the garden," said West Chac.
"Can you cut down trees?
I need a new corn field."
"I can cut trees," said the boy.
West Chac told him,
"Cut only little trees."

But the boy thought,

I can cut big trees.

He cut the biggest.

It began to fall.

"Help!" he said.

West Chac ran to help.

The tree broke the boy

in nine parts.

Nine times the chac sang

and the nine parts

went back together.

"You are not much help

cutting trees," said the chac.

"Can you dig yams?"

"Oh, yes," said the boy.

West Chac told him,

"Just dig the yams.

Do not look under them."

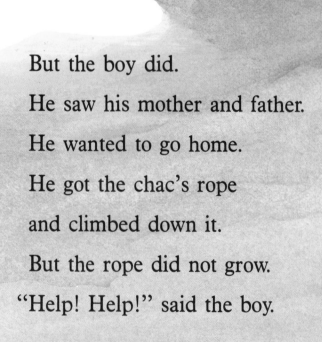

But the boy did.

He saw his mother and father.

He wanted to go home.

He got the chac's rope
and climbed down it.

But the rope did not grow.

"Help! Help!" said the boy.

West Chac had to run
and pull him up.
"I am always helping you,"
he said. "When are you going
to help me?"
The boy said, "Maybe you
should send me home."

"No," said the chac.

"I need help."

But the boy

thought only of home

and how to get there.

He took a black cloud
from the loom
and the bag of wind
to push it.
But he could not hold
the bag shut.

All the wind got out.
"Help! He-e-e-lp!"
he called.

West Chac ran
and got the wind.
He put it back
in the bag.
He stopped the cloud
and pulled the boy
back to the garden.
"You are no help at all,"
said the chac.

He pulled up a yam
and put down the rope
and sent the boy home.
But the boy's house
was turned around
and had no roof.
All the trees were down.

"I will have a big corn field now,"
said Father.
"It was the biggest wind
I ever saw."
Mother said, "All the turkeys
and ducks blew away."
The boy said, "I did that!
I made the new corn field
and turned the house!"
And he told them everything.

His father gave West Chac

many things

for helping the boy

and sending him home.

And when the corn

was ready to grow

and people called the chacs,

they gave West Chac something

to keep the wind bag shut.

Then West Chac had time to sit
on the turtle and sing with his friends.
"That boy was some help
after all," he said.